You Hold Me Up

You Hold Me Up

Monique Gray Smith and Danielle Daniel

SCHOLASTIC INC.

Artwork created using gouache, acrylic and pencil.
Cover and interior artwork by Danielle Daniel.
Author photo by Centric Photography.
Illustrator photo by Gerry Kingsley.

Printed in the U.S.A.

ISBN-13: 978-1-338-54136-6
ISBN-10: 1-338-54136-6

12 13 14 15 40 26 25 24 23 22

Scholastic Inc., 557 Broadway, New York, NY 10012

This book was written in the spirit of Reconciliation
and is dedicated to the children, families and
staff of Aboriginal Head Start programs.

—M.G.S.

To Melanie Hunt

—D.D.

You hold me up
when you are kind to me

when you
share with me

when you
learn with me.

You hold me up
when you play with me

when you
laugh with me

when you
sing with me.

You hold me up
when you comfort me

when you
listen to me

when you
respect me.

You hold me up.

I hold you up.

We hold
each other up.

Author's Note

In Canada, we have a long history of legislation and policies that have affected the wellness of Indigenous children, families and communities. One of the most impactful was Indian Residential (boarding) Schools. For over 150 years, Indigenous children (First Nations, Métis and Inuit) as young as five were taken from their families, communities and cultures and placed in Residential Schools. At these schools, abuse was rampant. The children were separated from their siblings, forbidden to speak their own languages or practice their culture, often fed little or rotten food and were denied basic necessities.

With this book, we are embarking on a journey of healing and Reconciliation. I wrote it to remind us of our common humanity and the importance of holding each other up with respect and dignity. I hope it is a foundational book for our littlest citizens. A book that encourages dialogue among children, their families, their care providers and their educators. At its heart, it is a book about love, building relationships and fostering empathy.

With respect and love,
Monique Gray Smith

Monique Gray Smith is a mixed-heritage woman of Cree, Lakota and Scottish descent and is the proud mom of twins. Monique's first published novel, *Tilly: A Story of Hope and Resilience*, won the 2014 Burt Award for First Nations, Métis and Inuit Literature. Monique's career has focused on fostering paradigm shifts that emphasize the strength and resiliency of the First Peoples in Canada. She is well known for her storytelling, spirit of generosity and focus on resilience. Monique and her family are blessed to live on Lekwungen territory in Victoria, British Columbia. For more information, visit www.moniquegraysmith.com.

Danielle Daniel is the author and illustrator of *Sometimes I Feel Like a Fox*, a finalist for the First Nation Communities Read Award, a finalist for the Blue Spruce Award, the winner of the Marilyn Baillie Picture Book Award, and a selection on the New York Public Library's list of most notable books of 2015. She writes and paints in Sudbury, Ontario. For more information, visit www.danielledaniel.com.